The Day
is Such
a Lady...

Col. Tom Cox, CAI

&

G. Kim Franz, Ph.D.

ISBN 0-9644276-0-5

Library of Congress Catalog Card Number: 94-93920

DEDICATION

To Those
Who Hold the Light
And
To the Few
Who are the Light...

Clara and Gregory B. Cox
Jane Ellen, Reva
&
Margaret and Bernard LaVern Franz

ACKNOWLEDGEMENTS

Thank you to
Maxim Graphic Services
for the cover design
and photo accurateness.

Thank you to Reva Cox
for editing.

This Book Belongs to:

POETRY & PHOTOGRAPHY

Cover
LASSEN NATIONAL VOLCANIC PARK

The Lady Speaks...

Lincoln City, Oregon	2
The Day is Such a Lady	3
Mt. Hood	4
Glad Lady	5
Trillium, Forest Park	6
A Fragrance	7
Bear Tooth	8
Lady Angel	9
Jonathan	10
A New Day	11
Mt. View, Idaho	12
Life's Beauty	13
Elegance	14

Reva's Secret...

Romance & Music	16
Reva's Secret	17
Duality	19
Yellowstone National Park	20
Racheal's Lessons	21
Racheal	23
Cascade Range Snow Stream	24
Blessings in Life	25
St. Helens, 1980	26
Celebrating Life	27
Singing Wishes	28

Loving & Life Dreams...

Mt. Hood	30
The Baker	31
Upper McCord Creek Falls	32
Life Paths	33
Long Beach, Washington	34
Dreams	35
Tides	36
Tides & Time	37
Olympic Range Forest Fall	38
Thanks	39
Frozen Multnomah Falls, 1980	40
Many Hands	41
Life	42

Living Streams & Giving...

Green River George	44
Hell-o Tree	45
Yosemite National Park	47
Orphan Tree	48
Give and Take	49
He Shared These Words	50
Oregon Coast	52
Simple Things	53
The Nightingale	54
Redwoods	56
The Mark of Time	57
Snow Bridge	58
A Secret	59

Little & Big Lessons for All...

Child Playing in the Sand	62
Six Million Reasons	63

Spirit   69
Grandson   70
Young Hearts   71
 Wooden Dolls   72
Child Doll   73
 Children   78
Our Children   79
The "Might Have and Could"   80

Lullaby of Winter...

 Ice & Waterfall   82
Winter Lullaby   83
 Silver Thaw   84
Dressed   85
 Swirling Waters   86
The Circle   87
 Mt. Rainier Region   88
Winter's Hand   89
Days End   90

Lace & Dusk...

 January Oregon Coast Sunset   92
Things Remembered   93
 Essence   94
Doc   95
 Yellow Stone Canyon   96
Canyons   97
 Columbia George Waterfall   98
Silence   99
Our Hope   100

The Lady Sleeps...

 Black Sands Basin, Yellowstone   102
To The Lady.....   103

The
Lady
Speaks...

The Day is Such a Lady

The day is such a Lady,
She is lost at what to wear:
I'll make a gown of Sunset
Braid some Moonlight in her hair,
A Rainbow 'round her tiny waist—
Blush her cheeks with Dawn,
Dance her into Stardust
Kiss her 'til she's gone.

Tom Cox, 1989

Glad Lady

At best we rest
In the deep dark night
Until we feel the face
Of morning light,

Shadows lengthen
Moments fall fast
Again, we dream
The Past will last,

Be glad, My Lady,
As each day is told
Life together
Is something to hold.

Tom Cox, 1991

A Fragrance

I love her fragrance Dearly
Of a long forgotten time;
When I met my Lady
All the world was mine,

I drank in her beauty
Our love was meant to be;
Her smile... lips... and laughter
Cast a spell on me,

Her young body next to mine
All dressed in silk brocade;
She asked to leave at morning-light
A sacred vow we'd made,

The years rolled up the scroll
My heart shall never rest;
Our love forever sealed in gold
With a locket on her Breast.

Tom Cox, 1991

Lady Angel

A gift to you, My Lady,
Of a kiss to Light your Soul;
Served on a Silver Saucer
Within a Golden Bowl,

My Lady, both young and fair
Sparkling eyes and sunny hair;
Be not afraid, Child of Light,
Angels watch thee throughout the Night.

Tom Cox, 1990

A New Day

With each new dawn, I wait for Light
My spirit is strong and swift in flight,

I share my brother's load along the way
Sing a Song of praise for each full day,

I walk along sea and meadows wide
My Heart grows whole on the other side,

For, I shall live long and share my bread
Wear Eagle feathers and ribbons Red.

Tom Cox, 1988

Life's Beauty

Before life's beauty I finally Kneeled
Over mighty mountains and flowered Field

Was it a Golden Dream with Silver Clasp
Or simply Silent Shadows... of the Past?

Within each Human Heart
There is a will to win
Sometimes to be Shut Out
Is to be softly...
Let In.

Tom Cox, 1989

Elegance

Winter came one cold bright morning,
Sweeping down the old dusty road
Blowing the leaves to rags

Winds touched the distant door
Greeting each soul
Room to room

I bartered for the day
Until darkness chased her home

Her long fiery hair
Threw flaming kisses to us all

In a simple sunset dream.

Tom Cox, 1988

Reva's Secret...

Reva's Secret

Reva whispered me a secret:
Songs of Belly, Breast and Thigh
Magic moments from the Past
Music, meant to Mystify,

Stories of Beaded Berry Baskets
Cedar sounds across a Yew Wood Bow
Long before words were written
To the beginning, the Legends go...

Language of Raging Rivers
High lakes and Mountain Streams
Hunter's Heart a Drumming
Within this Warrior's Dream,

Reva whispered me a secret:
Wood smoke raising in the Frost
Clear skies, Winter Noon
Ancient Melodies...
Sung under a Golden Moon,

Reva shows me Hidden Beauty
The Last is Greater than the First
Her Smile, the sweetest ever
Leaves me with... Endless Thirst,

Reva, I have only simple Gifts
Forest Flowers of Red and Blue
Wrapped in the Satin of my Soul
To Tie my Heart to You.

Tom Cox, 1986

Duality

To every Day there is a night
For every dark there is a light,

The rain doth smooth the curling fern
As the thirsty doe, a drink doth earn,

Wisdom leaps from branch to branch
To drum each leaf into a dance,

The single rose
A gift to hold,
To taste its beauty
Is to live Two-Fold.

Tom Cox, 1988

Racheal's Lessons

It is time for us to gather
To open the Silver Door;
I have some songs of Racheal
You have never heard before

I'm thankful for those early years
The ones filled with Never Ends;
The precious stones were gathered
The strong can learn to Bend

Racheal loves us All
Youth wastes Time on Take;
One should live to Give
Our tears for her too late

When She kissed me softly
It turned my soul to Gold;
It now no longer matters
That I am growing Old,

Some still wait on her
Listening for Her steps
Across the wooden floor...

Even in the darkness
She will come to us,
For my heart is on the door.

Tom Cox, 1987

Racheal

Racheal by the Roadside,
Her smile so Hot and Dry
Lips like Wild Cherry Wine
Eyes as Blue as Sky,

Her kiss did fade so quickly
Oh, I must bare the Sorrow,

To redeem the Heat
Of her Heart Beat,
I must dream
Inside tomorrow.

Tom Cox, 1988

Blessings of Life

As each day turns dark
Never to be retrieved,
Always remember
The many bright little things,

Glances from the heart
Smiles shared in rain,
Simple and kind thoughts
Walking without pain,

Now... Resting arm in arm,
Sipping on the clouds
Night surrounds these woods,
In silent mindful pause,

What was perceived as lost
In our spirit resides,
Joined to our hearts...
Very much alive!

G. Kim Franz, 1988

Celebrating Life

We are all a witness to
Significant life events;
Caring for each other
Strangers, family and friends,

Embracing personal faiths
Committing to love;
We celebrate this life
In rich harmonious song,

Monstrous mountains left to mount
Deep dark dungeons await;
But, we'll endure past our end
Touching hearts along our way,

Time is to be cherished
Clocks simmer, yet run strong;
So lets sit down together
And create a brand new song.

G. Kim Franz, 1993

Singing Wishes

Hear the tinkle of silver bells
From the old man's holly cart,
Ringing in a shower of songs
To dance across your heart,

A pocket full of diamonds
He flings into the sky,
To wink back some wishes
Just for you and I.

Tom Cox, 1990

Loving

&

Life

Dreams...

The Baker

He calls Himself a Baker
Which is far more than it seems;
Cakes, He makes with Magic Smiles
He decorates with dreams,

He cooks most any Order
Except for frowns or Frosted Fears;
No tools of Toil...
Happy Hearts
Sweetened by the years,

"I'll make you cakes and cookies
Pies and candy too!
The batter's all the same
It's made with Love for You."

Tom Cox, 1987

Life Paths

The days of our lives
Are like beads on a string
We know not what
Each new day will bring,

So let there be music in the Meadows
Songs in the Streams,
We each must walk
The path to our Dreams.

Tom Cox, 1989

Dreams

From my dreams, shall spring fresh flowers
You may thread them in your hair;
From my heart a robe of red
I ask that you would wear,

From my travels in skies of blue
I shall weave a silken sheet;
As a place upon which to rest
Remembering times so sweet,

From stars I gather bits of light
Lay them in a golden line;
Then 'round thy wrist, sealed with a kiss
My Love, 'till the end of time.

Tom Cox, 1993

Tides & Time

The ocean swims and swishes
Seeking newer lasting pitches,
Blending with the winds aloft
Life sails as youth doth learn to cross,

Endless mirrors of love and lust
Commitments made of lasting dust,
Shadows creeping towards the light
Time bleeding, weeping and growing nigh,

Seasoned grains are pearls in time
Threaded joys created, redefined
Present and past reside in mind
Pewter sparkles, silken... honed fine,

Youth is lost on the young and strong
Chartered characters, glow with each sun,
Morning aged and moonlit bays
Swirling tides, these crafted lives do sway,
With lasting memories of planet days.

G. Kim Franz, 1989

Thanks

How dear to my Heart
Those precious moments of Racheal;
A fond collection
Her smile within me,

A prayer just for You
Candled for your many journeys;
Should you cross a stream
That she has named Love,

Stop, my dearest friends,
And thank the burning stars above;
Blood red Heart she gives
And a Golden gift...

A Locket
To keep full measure
in the back
Of an old man's Pocket.

Tom Cox, 1987

Many Hands

Best wishes to All
As we journey on;
Though the miles may be many
We must still keep our Song,

Let good memories live forever
With Head and Heart let us Share
Remembering friends absent
Their Dreams we must Bare,

Best wishes to All
As we all journey on...

For friendships are cherished
Welcome, Indeed
It takes many Hands
For us all to succeed.

Tom Cox, 1988

Life

Life can be cruel and full of tricks
Remember, Love and Hate will never mix;
So live not with Burdened Breast
Nor, a Shackled Hand
Rather bless the Soul of your fellow man,

Cast your dreams upon a chosen star
It matters not how close or far:
But join those willing to explore
Use your Deeds, not Words
To open the Door,

And, when you wish upon a
Wondrous Morning Star:
Promise Always to leave
The Door of life... Ajar.

Tom Cox, 1988

Living
Streams
&
Giving...

Hell-o Tree

Hell-o tree, so grand and tall
What kingly tales can you tell?

"In years gone by when snails crawled
Birds once flew, as reindeer skirted by;
The air was pure and smelled like snow
River babbled at my toes;
Squirrely chatter, nut filled mouths
Charlotte wove luring silver clothes,"

Hell-o fir, what do you miss?
Many seasons gone and surely twisted,

"The frogs that croaked when sunset fell
Rocks once dressed in shining silk;
Eagles nesting in my braids
Youngsters pecking as insects played;
Uncle Knot - Knot once stood near
Aunt Coreless cones, tasted dear,"

So is it better with brush cleared mire...
Protecting you from lingering fire?

"I think not, the sun is hot
My old spotted owl has passed on;
Moose and elk are running scared
The mountain's tender way up here;
My kingdom's baking dry by day
I'm sad and lonely in the rain,"

Well, Douglas Emperor
What can we do?

"Think of me, as I think of you
With rights to live a fuller life,
Un-encumbered in soggy light
Drinking crystal dew watered ice,
Twinkling stars, no garbage strewn
Quit cutting down my Friends
I need them too!"

G. Kim Franz, 1990

Give and Take

Lumberman, Logger
Take this tree
To make a bow
For General Lee,

Shape it strong
Cut with the grain
Soft and smooth
For the Lady Jane,

Carpenter, Craftsman,
Do build a Chair
So, to rock my child
To Delaware,

Then, with Silver Spade
And trusted hand
Plant a tree back
In this mighty land.

Tom Cox, 1989

He Shared These Words

He wore a crown of iron, a sword of steel;
A silver chain with a family seal,
With words of thunder,
His eyes stared cold;
Upon his chest a mighty crest
An eagle trimmed in gold,

We met but once, on Life's lonely trail,
He shared these words that will not fail:

"Use well the moment,
Take it hour by hour;
Listen to Life's rhyme and rhythm
For they are your power,

Stay with deed and duty - -
Send only the arrow that is true;
Give each day a greeting
And it shall welcome you,

Everything has its purpose
One must seek,
If one is to find;
And, if you must fight,
Choose what is right,
Then bright stars shall reward your crown."

We met but once on Life's lonely trail,
He shared the words
That have not failed:

The thunder of His voice
The Jewels in the Eagle Crest
Shall... and will prevail.

Tom Cox, 1988

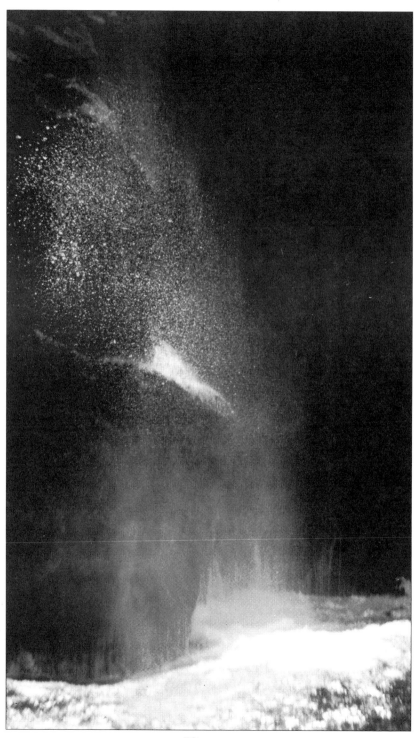

Simple Things

There is a charm in Simple Things
To feel the Wonder each day brings;
Hour - by - hour
Softer than Dewdrops
Upon a Flower,

Live each day Open
Without the walls;
Gain gentle
Wisdom
As
Darkness
Falls.

Tom Cox, 1987

The Nightingale

It's time to tell you a story
Sung by a Nightingale;
About a place of Magic
Flowers fragrant too,

You must trust in me
I will trust in you;
In this time together,
Beauty grows
All our dreams
Can come true,

I cleared a path
Pure as ermine Snow;
Friends will meet us there
The Silver Fox
The Golden Bear
The Nightingale too,

The Lodge at the Four Fountains
Is open to welcome us;
The wailing winds await
Life's fanfare just,

Climb upon your Silver Steed
For you must make this date;
Life is like the wines' sweet vine
Thirsty, growing by the lake,

It grows so strong
And then so tall;
Harvest always from the top clusters
Or pick no fruit at all,

Remember always our given Place
Where unknown tomorrow's live;
Before you ever think to take,
You must first learn how to give.

Tom Cox, 1987

Mark of Time

Sweet Rains of Opportunity
Shall ascend upon the Noble:
While the Winds of Wonder pass
Gently through the
Valley of Silence,

All that is good and true
Shall not be lost;
Rather, carefully passed on
To seed a new Beginning
Of a Golden memory.

Tom Cox, 1988

A Secret

This is a riddle
For the answer...
Do not peek;
Within these lines...
A secret lies
If happiness...
Is what you seek,

So many times I wonder
What is it...
We all fear?
It's who we are inside that counts
Not reflections in a mirror,

For a Stone is a Rock
Our Life, a Clock
The River, a Road

The Path of Purpose
Can be yours
When lived by a Code,

Fly right through the waters
On Silk and Silver Wings;
What is good...
Gets better
I know about these things,

Each day has a few treasures
So, hug them to your heart;
Remembers always,
Dearest Friend,

It's never too late to start.

Tom Cox, 1987

Little &
Big Lessons
for All...

Six Million Reasons

We have six million reasons
to be grateful each day,
Scars of the past...
Will not shroud our way;
All life experiences...
Were meant to be shared,
No time for depression
Loathing, despair,

We have six million reasons
to compare what we know,
Gaining in wisdom,
As the grains of time flow;
Abundant Blessings...
Teaching us now,
Traditions are many
Memories allowed,

We have six million reasons
to be seeking the truth,
Hopeful to change...
Man's trite horridness;
Clever and cunning...
Beyond brazenness,
Capacity for killing
And then to forget,

We have six million reasons
to be gracious and kind,
Yet, a lingering rage
Still remains deep inside;
Mobbing our spirit... it moves us on,
Mother-less, Father-less
Sister-less, Brother-less
Inside our consciousness,
The numbness resides,

We have six million reasons
to never forget,
Those poisoned years
Filled with relentless hatred;
Injustices far to great...
Much silenced through re-creating history,
Thoughts... Seeping slowly
Then releasing
Toxic mire of...
What some want to believe,

We have six million reasons
For staying well and alive,
Blessed by our traditions
No room for brooding inside;
Grateful to count... all the possibilities,
Life is a gift... so many dreams
Left to be dream
And realized,

We have six million reasons
to be actively socially heard,
Fighting against discrimination
And for tolerance;
Holding to the ethics...
A spiritual song,
Remembering always
To share peace and love,

We have six million reasons
to celebrate life,
Man has the ability
To seek what is right;
In spite of the pain...
God has given us light,
The choice of free will
To get involved
Healing other hearts
Educating the mind,

I have have six million reasons
to teach all that I know,
The words my father spoke,
Reside in my soul;
"We take only in death...
What we give away in life"
He whispered again... before he died,
"Material objects will not buy...
Peace of mind,
Education and knowledge...
Can change the tide,
Shalom, my daughter... continue the fight
You have made me proud,"
His breath drew nigh,

We have six million reasons
to be the best we can be,
We can work to make a difference,
As life is shorter than we think;

No one is to young or old...
To answer the call,
Creating peace
And justice
Intended ...for all,

Stand firm... For,
We all share six million reasons,
To live life to the fullest
Treasuring everyday;
Store no regrets... time slips away,
Keep the flame aglow
Love those who pass your way
God's beauty lives...
In the simple things
A touch... a hug... a kiss
A sunset on the bay.

G. Kim Franz, 1994

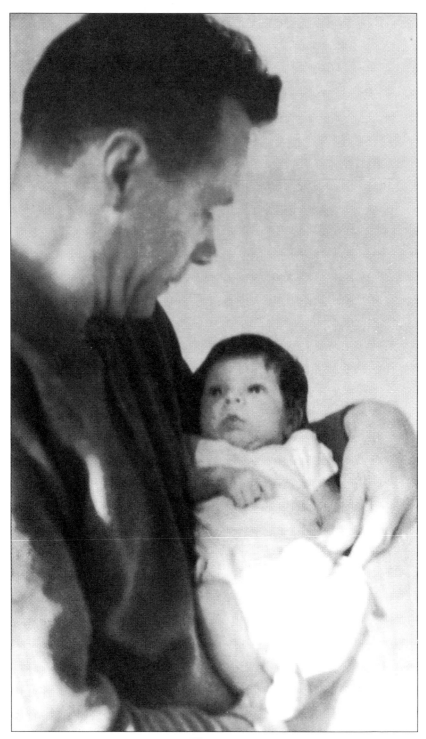

Young Hearts

Songs from those before Us
Lend life to our own Chorus;
Proud are we now
Who carry our name,

It is a sign
To see our sons and daughters
Grow strong and kind,

Eager young hearts beat fast
With Honor and Pride,

And, whose sweet spirits unwrap
Each new day...
As it is
A very Precious Gift.

Tom Cox, 1987

Child Doll

The parents
Where are they?
I see them not,
A father at home
At work or play
In a grave
Not at all...
He walked away,

Teenage mother
Weary and torn
Raising Child Doll
Hoping to fill
A void deep inside
To feel loved once more
Endlessly now,

Teenage Mother
Lonely with dreams
Wants the freedom
To come and go,
Do what she pleases

Or, so she believes...
Only to learn,

That Child Doll
Has many demands
Beyond being loved
Kept warm from cold
Playing grows tired
Illusions are shattered
Mirrored images of time
Moves on and on and...

With no education
State papers for aid
Where is the future
Teenage Mother once
Held near, even dear?

Child Doll grows up
And now takes flight
To rid herself of
Mother's plight,

Selling drugs
To buy new shoes
Child Doll wants more
To fill her void,

Seeking freedom
From relentless pain
Only to repeat
The same cycle of need,

So, Child Doll
With no place to go
Learns... like teenage Mother
That love will not
Conquer the poverty
Depression or lust
She's now with child
Deep in her guts,

Child Doll re-created
That which she knew
Subsidized housing
State aid
No education
Rats
Garbage for play
And
Violence and Rage,

"When will this end?"
You righteously ask,
I'm sorry to say
I think it will not
Our ignorance is bliss
Silences the past,

Had we found teenage father
And forced him to pay
With either time or money
For Child Doll's way
The difference would be,

A new social path...

But that's not the way we do it
Look at the past
We blame Child Doll
For getting pregnant
And in unison
Turn our backs,

If we really owned
Social responsibility
For life and its joy,
"A beautiful choice"
Then, not so easily
With... Acceptable
Rationally justifiable
Excuses,

Would we look the other way
As Father Child
Bows Out.

G. Kim Franz, 1992

Our Children

The rose is sweeter to the native son
Than to the one who named it well,

Who hears the Chimes the purest
Than he... who hammered the bell,

So... as each day is put away
Fear not the coming Night,

Remember, Good Deeds honored
Become the Stars of Light.

Tom Cox, 1989

The "Might Have & Could"

I met a man from a land...
He called it "Used to Be"
All of his Youth he spent
Roaming the "Once I Was"
But, he always took time
To sip some wine at the Inn of
"It Should Have Been,"

One of these days
In the morning of Time
There is a place
We both should Climb:
Two by Twice
Jump up
Go round:

First we start at my Home Town

Silver Moon, Golden Star
Here we are...
"In How Things Are."

Tom Cox, 1987

Lullaby
of
Winter...

Winter Lullaby

Up the tired and Tattered Foothills
Like shadows in a row
Stand rugged lines of gentle pines
Just waiting in the snow,

From the Mighty Mountains
Reach an old familiar hand
Crawling at the tree tops
And grabbing for the land,

Farewell, my Summer Beauty
From autumn arms you fly
Winter winds will lift your wings
To sing you a lullaby.

Tom Cox, 1991

Dressed

Frozen...
This Silver Lady,
Howling... Singing
The winds do blow,
Pure as a thought
Before it is told,
Dressed for a ball
Winter unfolds,

Chilled...
Dying summer flowers
Draped in snow,
Dancing soft mist
Between Emerald twists.
Laced in the ice
Cold Sunshine bright,
Crafted by Nature
A Perfect sight,

Her smile is wondrous
To the heart, soul and mind.

Kim Franz, 1993

The Circle

Stir the stone with simple love
Watch the ripples from above,

Shake down gently with full measure
To live life well is the treasure,

Those so wise shall hold a kindly light
To hearts whose path is cloaked by night,

The flame reflects from a distant hill
Though the Gift be gone
It encircles still.

Tom Cox, 1994

Winter's Hand

In these parts winter can come slowly,
Yet, the feel of it...
Cracks the Whip weeks before,

The leaves, like lost guests,
Depart for another year
Only a few are there...
To Welcome

The Old Man
Walking in grey tent Rain...
Still as Stone
Hawk-hooked Hands
Hair white as Bone
Is always there
With a Smile.

Tom Cox, 1987

Days End

Day's end is upon us
The edge of darkness near;
It spells safe shelter
For the dove and deer,

Soft is the silence now
That seeps throughout the day;
Sweet are the blossoms
Fresh flowers display,

A circle of time
Has closed and completed;
Songs of the season
Are restored and repeated,

May the fan of twilight
Conceal all your sighs
As star upon star
Arrives in the sky.

Tom Cox, 1993

Lace
&
Dusk...

Things Remembered

Song and story
From distant Lands
Home cooked meals
By my Mother's Hands,

A stone wall laid
Years before
The weathered house
With curtains tore,

Big front porch
With a squeaky door
Talons of Time
On the bare wood floor,

All send a message
That the Heart will Hear
Of Folks and Farms
I wish were near.

Tom Cox, 1989

Doc

Your beauty is in my soul
Warming the winds of time,

Never near or far way
Alone, in silent walk,

Beholding is your host
Angelic presence sought,

Memories aside,
I still miss your touch
Laughter...
Gracious thoughts.

G. Kim Franz, 1980

Canyons

Much of what was
Still is...
Much of what could be
Will not be...
Much of what has been
Was simply rough,
But, we faced this Valley
Knowing love,

I look to your stream
To carry me on,
I look for your wisdom
Nesting in light,
I look to your smiles
laughter and fun,
I look to your rivers...
Our last seconds... gone.

G. Kim Franz, 1976

Silence

I have a certain place
Known only to my eyes,
Sweet waters run forever
Tall trees to fill the skies,

My place and I are one,
From the beauty I cannot part;
Locked away from a stormy day
It's sewn into my Heart,

Ride with me on the Eagle's back
Between his golden Wings;
Fly to the edge of Heaven
And stay... till morning Sings.

Tom Cox, 1992

OUR HOPE

We hope that in the stillness
Of a once forgotten sun
The answers to life's mysteries
Is touched upon your heart,

For in this meadow of plenty
The famine is great
Varied and abundant
As far as the eye can see,

The sacred touch when felt
Is so... Subtle
That it stings!

Col. Tom Cox, CAI

&

G. Kim Franz, Ph.D.

1994

The
Lady
Sleeps...

To the Lady...

Sterling Qualities of Character
Strength and Honor
Are Her Clothing,

And...
Her Family and Friends
May well arise
To call Her Blessed...

Ordering Information

The First of Four Books

The Day is Such a Lady.................... $12.95

Racheal's Song................................. $12.95

  VISA & MASTER CARD ACCEPTED

Shipping & Handling 7-15% Pending Quantity

Five to Nine Books

15% Discount

Ten to Twenty-Four Books

20% Discount

Twenty- Five To One Hundred Books

30% Discount

To Place Order

MAIL TO: COX–FRANZ PRESS
PO BOX 6770
PORTLAND, OR. 97228

PHONE: (503) 248-9622
(503) 282-5027

FAX: (503) 335-0471
(503) 223-5506

Thank-You for the Order !